I Face My Love

Coemgen

Everush Books

I Face My Love
Copyright © 2010 Everush Books

ISBN 978-0-9778833-3-2
Library of Congress Control Number: 2009933331

Published by Everush Books

This book may be purchased at online booksellers. The book may also be ordered through retail book stores using the ISBN number: 978-0-9778833-3-2.

For you, my love,
my precious Dale!

May you forever find in this book
eternal renewal of our lifelong handfasting.

There dwels sweet Loue and constant Chastity,
Vnspotted Fayth, and comely Womanhood,
Regard of Honour, and mild Modesty;
There Vertue raynes as queene in royal throne,
And giueth lawes alone.

The Promise

If only I could find the word—
Would the word find me!

You saw me, loved me, made me.
Joyous, I promised speech.

Your word, my love, endures.

Prologue

I conceived this telling of these events while you slept in our motel room. The night before was a renewal of that earliest life we spent together. Now it is time to write of the preconditions to love. In my vision, you were whole, but I was pocked with islets of emptiness, the result of my infection and the false and mistaken steps I had taken in coping. Love as we conceive it is not possible if emptiness is not quarantined.

My love, I wrote those words four months ago, in our motel room in Victoria. I woke suddenly in the early morning, having slept for only an hour or two, after we had loved so beautifully. The imprint of your love was fresh on my soul and body, and these words came to me, with an insistence that was not to be denied. So, quietly and carefully, I got out of bed, went to the desk, and I scribbled those words onto a tiny piece of notepad paper provided by the motel.

They were intended to be the beginning of this book— and indeed they are!—but I intended to write much more that morning. I was planning to write for hours, being with you interiorly as you slept beautifully on the bed beside me—launching my barque into the sea with sufficient impulse that it could never be turned back.

But having written those few words, the pen ran out. I did not want to disturb you, possibly wake you, by digging into my packed case to find a new pen; so, I got back into bed. In the next three hours I thought about this book, how I would write it. It would be a gift for you.

I have kept that little notepad sheet always with me ever since—wanting to keep those words, that promise, close at hand: reminder of the promises I made to you long ago.

And I have taken that paper out, and read it, again and again, over these months. Until finally, now, I realize that it *has* to be. Now is the time—perhaps it's the only possible time—for this book to come to be.

You have needed me to come to you for so long, and I have needed that, too. You have needed me to come back to you, to find you again, to live with you permanently— day by day, moment by moment... You have always deserved perfection in me. I apologize for not having always given that to you.

Ah, those early days! I still remember us sitting at the dining room table, guitars and tape recorder nearby, as we took a break from practicing, that first summer when we were together. You were facing me, smiling as you licked and moved your lips sensuously down and up the popsicle, head tilted slightly down, your eyes looking up at me, watching me look at your lips, and your beautiful, teasing eyes, enjoying my reaction.

And every part of me *wanted* you so incredibly! Until finally I couldn't take it any longer, and a mock complaining loving needing "You!" burst from my heart and soul. And your smile broadened, then we collapsed into laughter and kisses.

I wanted so much to marry you, to be your husband, your partner, your friend, your lover for life.

Oh! I loved today, too. Your birthday! Being with you this way again, these special days! What we shared in our beginning is coming back again, as days spent together (just the two of us!) re-become our norm. Surely you feel it too?

Words are so much better than a photograph. Because when we read artistically crafted words we live the truth of the original moment; yet, we also bring that historical reality into our present, into ourselves right now. And its light shines like a beacon inside us, forever wakening us. Words are pure living.

I told you I would write. I promised that when we first met. So now, my darling, now I will take up my quill, and retell to you our story: the story of how I became yours, how I came to belong with you, to you, how you enchanted me, charmed me, with your grace, your strength, your beauty.

I knew then, and I know now, that the highest art is to love perfectly. I would do that for you today, in composing this book.

This book is not precisely what I conceived that early morning in Victoria, as you slept so beautifully. But, it tells the same story—the story that I always intended for this first book. It contains that vision of love and life.

For the most part, I will let the words of our beginning speak for themselves, revealing our love as it was, but also as it remains today, as it always will be, in its heart and core, in our centered being and life.

I begin by revealing the "me" who originally attracted—incredibly!—your love. Your appreciation of the words that came before you was a sign to me that you were the *one*. You see, I had always assumed I would never be able to share the words inside me with the woman I would come to love. You surprised me!

I feel so lucky, so blessed, that we are both still here, on this Earth, so I can speak these words directly to you, give them to you forever.

You will find that all of these words, the historical and the new, reflect your love and beauty. They would never have come to be had you not loved me with such constancy and perfection, from eternity. That kind of love changes people—indeed, changes all nature:

> *Such is the powre of loue in gentle mind,*
> *that it can alter all the course of kynd.*

So now, my love, I take up my quill, and begin: transcribing what was into what is and always will be.

12 November 2008

Blood and Silence

Cygnus

Emblem of sorrow, by the serpent pricked:
Double-eyed ever she flies.

The Seaswan

That morning
I reflected sunglazed upon the dewdrop
Knowing it was true.

But sunrisinghigh
Sucked all away
Left me nakedparched clinging to
Diffused soulvapors irretrievable:
I burned in black light.

Now
I retire:
I will bathe in the sea and hope that
I like the grimfaced
Seaswan who unheeding plunges
Overvulnerable whiteness into that
Graygrained saltwetness will
Neither drown nor die for thirst.

Sea-Things

Cold restless shapes,
Armies on patrol,
They brush me

Or swallow me whole, and settle,
Amoeboid,
In the dark.

The Leaves Are Changing

the leaves are changing
color
      softly, slowly,
                    undiscernibly,
yet,
      tangibly:

      green
         into yellow
               into orange
                  red
brown,
      into black

what splendor marks their flight
      into
      death

Nova

I burst upon the night-deep sky,
Streaming star where there was none;
Now my life is swallowed by
The dark and scatter of my blood.

The Bleeding Man

On this plain, grim desert fringe,
Burnt, cracked portal fronting Death,
Lies the bleeding man, alone,
A thousand miles from home.
Twenty years he fought the bloodless
Fiend, who parried his assaults
For sport, fending without shield;
He strode boldly, defiant,
Feeling with each inconsequent lunge
And swipe the power bleed from him.
Now he swoons, old man at last,
Frenzied heart jetting life from him,
Pumping all onto craving sands,
While bleached sun sears his parched cheek.

Hero's End

The fighting's done, the battle unwon,
But the severed heart beats on.

The Severed Heart

I am a severed heart,
Bleeding toward my death;
My body's ripped apart,
I've but this voice left.

A modern man I was,
Suckling science to my breast—
Till it became a monstrosity
And wracked my house to shreds.

I fought the bloodless fiend
With glittery sword and shield;
The battle was but dream,
Played out in fancy's field.

I chased him cross the plains
And watched him drown at sea;
Then he became the cliffs
That towered over me.

I chased the bloodied black fiend,
Lest others might his words attend;
But my weapons were mere fancies:
Against pure logic they could not defend.

Beware the fiend and all his deeds,
For I believed, and now am dead.
This voice is but my spirit's dream,
The words of the rose above my head.

The Unclasped Hand

Blood drips from the unclasped hand
Dribbling down the cold gray stair.

It's waiting there: the pickled flesh,
Of a man who was your death.

Alphabet

All Being Creates Day
Every Falling Gathers Hearing
In Joining Knowing Living Makes Name Of Prayer
Quiet Revealing Sighing The Union Void
World X Yes Zero

The is the Father.
Of is the Son.
In is the Holy Spirit.

KEVIN: Knowing Every Void In Name

He knows that words are little nothings that divide the
world into pieces.

In the Beginning

In name, the hearing earth begins every gathering. In
name, name into name gathers. God of day created
revealed Earth—all the Earth's days. The hearing Earth
has ears all voicing every name's sign...

God's Name

God's name is I AM.
All that is is from Eternity.

Fragment from a Day when Visions Were Seen

O sing me of the everush!
Tipping sing, Uinverse,
Every hush uttering!

... everrings ...

heards
words of birds
burst

my head
a
heart:

HEAR "I AM"
EVER THESE WORDS
ARE THE ART

Universe

The Universe is meant to be a song:
one song.
One poem.
Uni-verse.

The World: it is each of us inverse:
our souls expressed
into material being:
u-in-verse: You-in-verse.
A song made of our lives.

Earth

Earth means Ear:
we are listeners, all of us.
Listeners to the light,
to the words life
whispers in our hearts.

Earth means Hearing.
Earth means Hearth.

Earth means Art:
our lives are our Art.
They are our Creation.

God gives us to create the universe.
It is what we make it.

God makes us.
We decide who we will be.
Our decision makes the Universe.

Within and Without

There is no without that has not been within. All that is before us has been forged within, and mirrors that within in all its complexity. What I experience in the world, what I see and hear and smell and taste and touch, is the ever changing image of all that is behind me, that is, history.

History? His story. Who's story? Man's story. The phenomena of the world are images forged since the beginning of time in the souls of men. Look: that hawk who circles stoically above the desolate bare-treed hill: how is it that he has arrived there? Just so have similar hawks circled before the eyes of men for millenia upon millenia. But not quite so, for their hearts were different. This particular hawk you and I see today is but the son of those thousand others, and not identical with them. For they were the phenomena of our fathers' worlds, and circled hilltops made in the image of our fathers' hearts, their within, which included our own but in potentia.

But how did there come to be any hawklike thing? What of that first hawk, from whom all others descended, the hawk that Adam first saw? Surely it leaped from his heart into the phenomenal world the moment he felt it stir and gave it its name! Originally the Word had implanted it there, and hawk and heart had been one, and nameless. Who knows how long it had circled those desolate reaches within his soul and beyond his vision, crying out to him, before finally he took notice? But in naming it he set it free: what had existed but in potential suddenly became reality, an actual phenomenal entity that could be seen and heard and remembered, all because of the word. Man had set the hawk and his heart apart, with but the word in between, and indeed his heart then was hawkless, and hollowed. The Word had been fractured and a manword made: a space between two that had been one. And time had begun.

14

What I see before me is an ever changing image, image of the life of man. For space and time are born of words: the expanse of space is but an expanse of words, a perceptual projection composed in language, in emptiness, and all distance is but the disjunction between man and his phenomena, which once were one in the Word.

Look at the world, and look at man. See the outer edge, but too the inner. The outer edge we "see" only with the aid of radio telescopes, instrumentation—that is, in theory. We "see" the edge of the universe, the edge of matter, and it recedes from us at the speed of light. What is it that we find there? Nothing but the rattlings of that bang which marks, in theory, that innermost edge of the within—namely, the Beginning. In the outermost, most unreachable edge of space is found the image of the nethermost, most unknowable edge of time. Is it any surprise?

In man lies all history: the past, which recedes within him as he lives his paltry Earth life, an inward movement reflected in the outward expansion at the speed of light of his phenomenal world, whose edge appears equidistant from him regardless of where he chooses to fix his gaze, that distance equal to the distance a ray of light would travel in the time from the theoretical beginning of the universe to the present—equidistant, as though the "Big Bang" had occurred right here, on Earth, in the hearts of men, so many billions of years ago, when Adam spoke that first, fatal word.

There is no without that has not been within. And there is no within that lacks potential to become an imaged without. Man occupies the centerpoint, and all nature is formed in his image. That's his story.

Radiant Star

Radiant star,
You are my sight,
Endless streaming
In the night;

And I'm a glass
That but refracts
The life you are,
The world you make.

Silence Is Your Name

Silence is your name,
Silence the name you gave me;
But bless this broken totem
(Round which ragged worlds have gathered),
For I am a fallen man,
My 'I' a fallen world.

O sweet silent wonder,
Let words gather and be still
As hushed they once whirled in awe
Round their living sun, and breathe
Into me your whispering dew:
Make me, dear Lord, anew!

Body

The body is a garden infused with a sliver of awareness.

Ruined "I"

In the dark wood of my soul,
I came upon myself:
a letter "I" made of stone,
in ruins:

prostrate,
cracked,
brittle,
wind-pocked,
weatherbeaten.

Vegetation growing around the base,
eyeless worms squirming beneath
the wet, mudded, supine form,
bugs crawling on the top and sides,
acid lichens dissolving its exposed surface.

Cracked and worn such that
it could never stand again.
Were any to try to raise it, stand it up,
it would fracture irrevocably,
collapse and crumble into
dry stony pieces
and dust.

Visions

You and I live halfway between our soul worlds and the world most people call the real world—and so, we have visions. We see the shallowness of the structures people call real. I see the shallowness even of things like physical trees, rocks, etc.—I mean, I understand how soul trees, and soul rocks, which are fluid like the entire real soul world—become solid to some extent—yet I feel the trees in my soul living inside both my body and the tree's body when I gaze at them in meditation.

Everything most people call real and solid and obvious— all those structures exist because human beings have conformed their thinking to the existence of such structures for centuries, for millenia. And our minds are like glasses—the light from our souls is refracted to create those structures everyone calls the real world. And after centuries of this, the mental structures finally banished all fluidity, calling it superstition, and claiming there is no such thing as magic. And people believe this; so, the world they perceive is a conglomeration of detached, spiritless "objects"—the structures—

Thus, they are blind to the interior rivers that compose your life and mine. They see only with the glasses our century has placed over our eyes—like Sylvia Plath's bell jar. Yet the bell jar, and the eyes within it, they do not see—they see only the distorted, yet supremely logical, "real" world.

You and I belong to an earlier age—one prior to the complete engulfment of the exterior world by logical structures. Or—in seeing those structures while also feeling the eternal river within us—we are among the few who can make a living future for this world.

So many people have lost their inside, and are scattered across the spiritless world!

18

Love Is Sufficient

Our love is always sufficient for today. Never, when we judge the past, do we feel like our lives have been a success—we see wasted years, so many things we could have done and should have done. But—as we both know—"could have" and "should have" do not really exist—since in the present moment we cannot feel the weaknesses of the past that have grown into this moment's strength. So—judging the past is useless. And judging the future is equally useless.

In judging the past we weigh memories of failings against our present strength, and we forget that the failings were a means for revealing to ourselves the need for the strengths we now have. Without the failings, would we now be strong?

And looking to the future, we hold up today's weakness against projected images of future needs, and tell ourselves "it's impossible, we just can't do it"—forgetting that love turns every weakness into strength and power in its time. In its time, when it's needed, but not before.

It's like the mystics, who always seemed to find that, when they were in their most desperate moments, when needs seemed hopelessly unfulfillable, they would turn, and suddenly find exactly what was needed right at their feet—given to them, from who knows where.

So it is with us. When we need, our loving will engender the answer to our need. And where will what we needed have come from? From the love within us, from beyond the point where all life is infused into us, into our souls; from the beginning of the world, the beginning of time.

Plans

We both felt so strong—like life was giving us what we needed when we needed it. Life does that for all who choose to live in this moment. It is those who plan, and stick stubbornly to a plan made up of a moment which no longer exists—it is they who end up needing and unable to provide for their own needs. Because they have aimed their lives down a personal vision of the future, and when they travel into that personal vision heedless of where the path of true life lies—then, they need. Because the only thing anyone needs is life.

And no momentary vision can fix life—because each vision is real only for the moment when it occurs. And, if one tries to limit life to that vision—then contact with life is lost, and life itself is lost.

Let's not make plans, and wound the present, today, with limiting visions of the future. One who lives always today always lives. And so we will live. And, when we need, life will give us the answer. Life will say to us: "I see you have a need. Here. Take this path. This path is the answer to your need."

Ghosts

I am afraid of the ghosts inside you. Just like you feared the ones inside me.

But if we live together there are no ghosts. Because the life in us is so much brighter than any ghost—and ghosts are nothing more than emptinesses that fabricate words into expression by conforming their emptiness into the inverse image of reality—and so they speak emptiness into us, if we stare at them instead of turning to the fountain, whose light obliterates all shadows. And ghosts are visible only when we stare into the dimness of our own shadows.

And if we stare into the skies all around us—where are the ghosts there? They live only in our shadows—inviting us to forever live an existence where we are imprisoned by our self—a stone cast upon the shore, while the river flows onward apart from us.

That's all that ghosts do—they make us transfixed on our self—and everything they say becomes a self-fulfilling prophecy—because with every faith we put in their worlds, they lead us farther from the stream, and deeper into our own night.

Death and Life

Only death addicts us; life is freedom.
Only life can melt away death.
Only what is real can scatter what is unreal.

Emptiness 1

What is emptiness
but a spot in the universe
where life should have been—but isn't?

Emptiness 2

We cannot give by creating emptiness in ourselves. All we can do is cover up a valley of sorrow—but at the cost of creating an emptiness that is greater than what would have been suffered had we simply lived the highest possible love we could, and given that love in the moment of need, and forever.

We cannot smooth over valleys of sorrow without creating a greater sorrow and uncertainty that shadows our entire life, because love that would have been had the sorrow been traversed is not—and the lack is felt: an emptiness that seems to have come from nowhere—yet is truly felt.

If we turn away from the sorrow, by turning away from the love—surely we also turn away from the joy—and leave a life that is flat—level, but unfulfilled.

Please—love everything that you know is true. Please don't turn away and say "It's impossible." There is only one love. And that love has no limits, except for those we erect ourselves, as roadblocks in our lives and the lives of everyone we love—beyond which no love may penetrate—and within which all emptiness arises.

Emptiness 3

And emptiness is the only enemy we face in this world. And an undefeatable enemy at that—because it is nothing but absence of what should be there, filling the universe: life.

Emptiness has no being, so how do you fight it? Every time you reach out to touch it, you die, and the part of you that touched it is no longer there, living as a part of your being.

It's suicide ever to willingly reach out for it, that's all.

Sacrifice

And even love is confused and disoriented when Life commands that love be sacrificed, even for love. Because love does not understand the division of this world, and how love can possibly seem to be at odds with love—and how even though love itself is one, the spaces between people can be unbridgeable—and how people can suffer in weakness of will to love, and die rather than love.

The world is stupid, materialistic, and idolatrous. Our hearts know what change has taken place, and what it means.

Sacrifice.

The river had flowed in a certain direction, and now meets there an obstacle, unpenetrable, unmeltable. And it swirls around the obstacle, a great dark boulder in the riverbed—and the waters are confused. For the waters, at their creation, at the beginning of time, had been given a desire, and a strength, to fill that spot in the riverbed, with love and hope and life. Yet the world has made at that point an unpenetrable obstacle.

And so, the waters turn away—but not without confusion, and lack of understanding. The love that would have been: how can it understand?

Find a new home for it. Call it. Ask it to come, to stop swirling about the boulder it cannot penetrate. Tell it to come with the river itself, and not cry over what could not be. Tell it to come and sing with us, and love the love we give one another. Ask it not to tarry, and endlessly swirl and touch the edges of darkness it cannot bring to life.

The Tree

I walked in the rain, and I looked at trees. And one tree in particular spoke to me of everything that was happening to us, and of life, and of faith, and of sacrifice, and of the perfect victory of life in the midst of apparent "un-life."

It was a tree that was close to the hospital—and because it was too close to the building, yet also too close to the road, many of its limbs had been cut off. And as I gazed up at it, it seemed like no matter what, no matter how many limbs had been cut off, that tree had still gathered itself in, all its energies, and sprouted new limbs. It had faith!

And it was a very ugly tree, perhaps. It had no symmetry. And one of its main limbs that had been allowed to grow was simply chopped away at its halfway point—so that branches, a few anyway, sprouted off of it, but its own reaching was denied.

And I just looked at it—and the rain was falling. And I was standing there in the rain looking at this ugly tree that was so beautiful to me, so full of the faith and the life I wanted to feel inside myself, and give to you. And I wanted to be like that tree—strong and faithful—reaching into life and glistening in the rain. Dormant for now, yet gathering its energies and preparing to sprout new life next spring. And its leaves would turn beautiful colors and fall to the earth in autumn. And the tree would have lived and grown—just like it always has. And always will. It will live and grow, no matter what branches life cuts off of it.

I wanted to be like that tree. For me, and for you. Because I knew that that tree lives every life that God gives it to live. And I wanted to be that way, and live every life inside me—so that I could be what you needed me to be yesterday. So that I could love you perfectly, which was all I wanted to do.

And I did love you perfectly, at first. But then I failed you and myself—and turned to a game instead of life. And stopped being like the tree. And willfully tore off one of my own branches. And stopped loving you perfectly, because the branch that I tore off is one that would have said to you "I love you."

Something in me wanted to be vicious, to dare life to try to hurt me. I knew none of it could stop me, or touch me, or hurt me. And none of it did.

But it was the viciousness itself that ended up murdering me, and cutting off that branch that you needed and I needed last night.

I just had to fall. I don't know why.

Heartless Bleeding Man

Heartless bleeding man hears foaming waters, waves beating, tolling incessant time. White sea spray salts his open wounds, now parched. And he is awake to pain and memory: a cavern in his chest where once life was.

Strange spectacle: he sees it now, alive still, but there, by itself, beyond his reach, alone: his own heart excised, ripped out, flung away, wasted on the sand, to die its own death while he, numbed, watches. Frantically, ferociously, it pumps away, jetting its dark deep life stream onto vacant sands. Blood bubbles first, boils, then is sucked down. But not without a trace: grains dyed scarlet, stained with life, memory retained.

He watches, oblivious to the cavity within him, his own heart beating into death, frantic thrusts now quieting, weakened toward somber rest. And blustering winds blow rising sand into his interior abyss, around the silenced heart, burying all. His own memory fades as he watches, life's blood exhausted, life work aborted, a life complete yet undone.

Taboo

There are some questions for which the least untruthful answer is silence. Denial is a lie. Yet, to summon an image of darkness that wanders only the void of the past (because it has been put to death) into a fully lit living and growing present, is to counterfeit that present (by creating new darkness where light is meant to be)— hence, to sin.

Once lost, light can never be recovered fully. A speck endures, shriven calcification of soul, spacetime singularity speaking in silence: "Someone died here." Graven inlet, it always will be findable if one searches, even amid utterly reformed born-again existence. And if one looks deeply into it, as into a backward-pointing lens, probes with it, beckons, stirring quieted pools of nothingness, voided darkness can be witnessed, made visible, and, should faith falter (which it mustn't), wakened.

Our lives, indeed, are fragile. All love is. This moment only is real. What would we have reality be? Surely the only life-sustaining possibility is to blind our eyes to all darkness, past and potential, to let the present well into being and fill all existence with its new light, light that has never before been seen or experienced.

And apologize for instantiation of taboo, this void of silence.

Awareness and Namelessness

Only that which proceeds from awareness and returns by nature to namelessness is possible; all else is illusion.

The Garden Stair

1

I have just realized that I must begin writing this down, everything that is happening, everything we are feeling and finding in this love. Because—so, so much is being created, and images formed of such beauty—images of heaven, the Beginning, where all life is eternally created.

2

Nothing has ever been so perfect. I have felt a kind of perfection flowing through me and into the world, out to the trees and the clouds and the stars; but never before did I feel it being met with and becoming one with another river.

And my whole body was transformed, and so wedded to my soul, by the gentle flowing of your life into me. Before, I had experienced all flowing outward and a weddedness of my soul and my body and the world—but, never before life pouring in the opposite direction, into my soul, but through my body first.

3

It was all a reaction from an earlier pattern—of running from every darkness—especially my body—until I felt myself totally engulfed, swallowed by this terrible, disgusting *thing* that had even begun to steal away the "I" voice in my consciousness. It had begun to speak to me in that way, calling itself "I" and me "you"—because I had run so far away. And it was as though in the act of looking at the outside world I was peering through a long tunnel of flesh, my body—and it wasn't me anymore, this body. It was something else—and it was going to kill me. The sky was going to fall in on me, and the little tunnel to the outside world was going to collapse, and I was going to be obliterated, engulfed totally by this raging thing.

4

You are free. If you must flutter away, then I will stay here and make a song of all the flowers you have given me. And it will be a song about my love who went away across the fields, but left me with a flower—an entire world, really. Because she said "I love you." And "I love you" never dies. You saw how it could never die for me once I had said it to someone. I died all around those words, but the words themselves never died—because what's real cannot die—it doesn't even know there is such a thing as death—which there isn't, really.

If you go away, you have already given me that: "I love you." And you have given me all those times when you held me close and made me one with myself again—for the first time since my childhood.

And you have given me my name, Kevin, so beautifully whispered. You have poured love into my soul, and the love you poured into me has carried that word, my name.

5

Your world is smaller than mine when we are separate. My world extends across time and space and is full of emptinesses. And your world is a heart and a sun that lives and moves across the universe—a star.

6

I am different from you in that way. I am not afraid. I am so scattered over the universe, that whenever I find a piece of myself I instantly want to give it to you. Because I have seen you take everything I've ever given to you, and hold it up before you, and look at it, and suddenly it's beautiful. My whole tattered existence is suddenly beautiful in the light that shines into me every time we touch, whether the touching be music, or talking, or laughing, or gazing, or touching with our bodies (which is really all of them)—the light from your soul pours into me, and all my life on this earth, that clothing, is made beautiful.

But what do I give to you? I love you, that is all. I want to give you every part of my world that might inspire blossoms in your world.

7

I know that all time and being is here right now. I know that history is just an image—a backward projection of realities that are here, now, inside us—an attempt simply to make them visible. And I know the future is such a silly idea—as though all that is isn't here yet. The idea of the future is a result of spiritual blindness—the things are already there, inside us, in the world—we just can't see them—so we hope for a future present when they will be visible.

I know that God is Imagination, and I know that you are so totally in touch with that life that no one understands you and everyone thinks you run from things—from the so-called "real world."

You go where God/Life/Love/Imagination carries you— all the saints are like that: butterflies. Or, as Thomas Merton saw it: like little birds flying very fast, not knowing where they are going, or where Life is going to carry them...

I am happy every time you say "We'll lose days"—and I was even happier when you said "We're going to lose years"...

8

There are times now when my soul must go into fasting—because you are not here... But I am not a good monk, and sometimes my fasting turns to despair.

And you too have doubts sometimes. But do you really have doubts when you are with me?

I don't say things sometimes. Sometimes I just feel so warm and beautifully inspired, and the light I am feeling is so beautiful, but also so silent. Like that poem that I wrote. I feel Silence sometimes. At my highest moments I always feel it—so awesomely beautiful—the beginning of all words—the life that lives at the heart and core of every beautiful book—it is silent, that Life. And the words are just an attempt to portray the beauty of that Silence. That is Eternity: Silence. Yes, there are sounds in the Garden—but the sounds are pure music, and the image they convey is that of the awesome Silence which is the beginning of all and which contains all.

And the immanent and the transcendent are the same Imagination, don't you see? Evelyn Underhill made me see that both are real—but for me, for everyone, I guess, who ever truly reaches that Life, the most real is that moment when all distances are banished, and Life simply is and Imagination is Everywhere—speaking every language! And everything is life and all words are one. And the only word I can think of for all those languages speaking all those words which are one is: Silence. As in "sigh"—because the silence sighs into and through the universe, and becomes all these words, all these birds. That's what my image of words was: birds. Flying out from within me to create the universe. And the universe was a U-in-verse because it was an inverted me, me inside out, and it was me put into a poetry that I could see (in "verse")—and it was also a union-voice because it was all words at one in making all...

Still I should say more, I know. But my quiet is truly felt so often when I am near you—I just want you to feel everything I am feeling, and words seem so distant compared with touching. Those words seem more real to me at those moments... Touching words...

9

The doors that I told you about. It is you! You opened them and walked into my room. And at first I didn't know you were there. But what I noticed was that the doors that I had struggled with for so many years—trying to shut them and keep them shut—those doors began to melt away, and I was no longer struggling with them. It wasn't that I had successfully closed and locked them—that would be impossible—but, rather, the doors themselves, along with the struggle to close them, melted away—and new doors appeared, on the other side of time, the other side of my room. And you were there, with me. And I saw you.

I had dreamed of knives long ago. The beastly darkness that was trying to engulf little "me" was throwing knives across the emptiness at me standing on my little island. Most flew by me, but one cut into my arm. And I looked at it, but felt no pain—just numbness.

I called that enemy "my body"—and now I wonder—was it not the other way around? Were not those dreams the pain-stricken cries of my body and passion, those innocent ones who the other me wanted to be rid of entirely? Who was the demon in my disintegrated self? Was it not that intellect—which so relentlessly pursued its goal that it very nearly fractured itself into tiny bits along with the rest of the world, its world, my world?

10

That poem, those lines—that is what I always wanted, but thought I'd never find. I thought I would always have to be the seer. And yet, I knew that somehow—I knew that a perfect lover would see me entirely. I just believed that it was impossible, that I would never find such a person because—perhaps she didn't exist. So I planned on living alone—and struggling with the doors and my unkind God.

I cannot believe that. But that makes us so much the same—I too have harbored a world inside me that could never be shared. And I too have waited and longed for one who would gently touch me there, and reach into me with her love—and unlock all the doors until finally all of them vanished.

When we are close, and I look at you in awe—that's what it is—awe—that you are here, in the center of my universe. That somehow you have come to me, from beyond the farthest edge of the universe, beyond all the stars and the galaxies, beyond all space and everything that can be seen with our eyes. It is with awe that I look at you, into you—awe that you somehow managed to penetrate all of that universe and be here, with me, at its center, watching it all be created.

And here we are, like the pillars of the temple; like the oak tree and the cypress. And the winds of the heavens dance between us and through us, like a moving sea.

Here we are, at the beginning of time, watching the world be created!

11

The symbol of my love for you is contained in the word wedding. That is all I desire—to be wedded to you in every way—to be wedded to your freedom—which means to stand with you always. You said yesterday you felt yourself one with me, after all our talking and crying and wondering. And last night I told you I want to love you perfectly in all ways. And you told me that you feel so free, and that you felt that my love loves you in being who you are, and in dancing wherever the moment takes you. It is so so true. That is so much how I love you...

You are so wrong when you feel that the swan cannot love the butterfly. Forever the butterfly will be dancing in the air—and the swan is heavier, and slower to respond—but that does not mean he cannot love and respond and understand the butterfly's dance. He loves always. He responds sometimes not quickly enough— and understanding is perhaps the slowest of all, because sometimes love makes it possible for him to respond, even though he does not yet understand...

12

Books are no longer highest for me. Because finally I am living a love that is beyond any love that any book I ever write could adequately convey. You have changed me so—or, rather, your love has lifted me to a higher level in my own self—into a world I always knew should exist, but which I now realize never could exist without intimate love and sharing. We share everything, don't we?

How is it possible that you have reached me? I am still so often amazed. When you touch me it is so real. You are so at the center of my being. When we are close, and you touch me, and I touch you, it is like the entire universe resonates with our love—and I am meeting you so deeply inside myself, and so close to the source of all life within us... And I just know that I love you and that love is so much more than I ever imagined it could be—so, so much more real and full of Life, the exact Life I have always read about and which I wanted to find through writing—that Life has become the world I live in, and is no longer a world I must strive to create out of myself. It was such an illusion to think I could create that world, that Life, out of myself alone. So conceited a conception, for so conceited a world (the one I lived in then)...

And it is like the egg and the sperm, only in reverse. Because you have traveled from the outside into and through my world, making it fertile all along the way, until finally you reached the center and turned me to face you—and our love was consummated. Conception.

And that is enough. That can never be lost.

13

I need you to find me—not just have me try to find you.

We are apart, and I go astray, and because you are not here to correct me at the first moment, when a single word from your lips would turn me once again toward where you really are—because you are not here with me, and because I am still trying to find you, I end up in the wrong place. And what I say to you the next time we meet is wrong.

But you abandon me if instead of trying to find me, and trace the trail of my wrongness, and find how indeed it was nothing more than a mistaken attempt to find you even without you being here—if instead of trying to find me, you stand and pass judgment on me, then turn away—I am not perfect. I need you to come to me too, especially in those moments when in trying to find you I have ended up losing you.

14

I have never put this much energy into life before—and I'm not really strong yet—not as strong as I know I could be if you could just believe what I want—and not turn away from me whenever I fail. Because when you do that, you lay the burden on me of finding you again at a time when I am lost myself. And when I say things looking for you, and they sound lost because I am lost, you say "You sound like you feel guilty. You don't have to say that." And you do not believe in me. It is true, I don't know what I am saying at those moments, because I am lost. But I am trying to find you—and sometimes I feel like you are simply standing somewhere judging me—turning from me because I have not found you, yet not trying to come to me on your own. Either I have to somehow find my way to your world, or our worlds will never be one. And every time I fail—

My intuition is not always strong. Sometimes you will have to reach out and cover me with your love, in knowing that all I want is everything that you want, even though I am unable to express it at that moment—even though I seem to be expressing the exact opposite of what I have said I believe in and what you know you believe in.

This life—these separations put us so out of phase with one another so often. I have never felt life pulling me so far up then letting me fall so far down.

15

That is the new life that I hope our visions for the future point to. A dawn. A walking into the sun. And the second vision I had—of you within me, like my own soul walking into my world.

16

All I've tried to do here is to love you. That is all I have wanted to do for my entire life, really. To love you. You are all my dreams fulfilled, and always will be. You are the mirror of my life. If I look across the ocean, and see that you have fallen, I know that it is because I too have fallen, only I hadn't yet realized it. And if I see you flying across the sky, among the stars, then I too am lifted into the sky, and I too fly among the stars, and we become a beautiful constellation both in each other's eyes and in the eyes of God—and some day, too, we will be beautiful in the eyes of all the world, though now it may chastise us.

17

You tell me I do not love you.

I say something that is wrong, that isn't what exists in my soul—and immediately you are so far away—and no matter what love in me searches for you, I cannot find you, because the false words have made you an island, and you see everything I do through the lens of the false words—and everything I do is distorted for you—and you are so sure it's all just a game, an experiment—and that I really feel nothing, that I'm incapable of loving someone.

18

If you ever went away from me, it would be because you had constructed a theory. And I know you could do it. You have all the evidence you need. You've seen every darkness and every lie—and it would be so easy for you, if you just looked away from me for a moment, to convince yourself that it has all been nothing more than lies, just like all the other lies that have been a part of my life/death. Because lies can only make death. There's too much evidence, too much past. And all you have to do is not pay attention to the love I am trying to express in the present moment. And you can do that simply by saying: "I've read everything, even what you've written for me, and it's the same. I know it's all lies, so I'm not going to listen to anything you say with my soul. Only with my mind. Because I know you *believe* you love me, but I know you don't really, because you can't." You can listen to me with your ears and your mind, but not with your heart and your soul. That's all it will take for you to be convinced, and surround yourself in a theory, and never feel my love.

Oh, I am dying!

And you will have your world: self-contained once again.

19

And finally we danced the slow dance. And you held me so, so close! And I felt myself wanting only to hold you. And I felt you so close to me, and you were holding me so tight.

And I was afraid, because of what was happening— because I felt myself desiring you physically—and I was

40

afraid that if you felt that, that you would be angry with me, and walk away very angry.

And you looked at me at the end, and you were so beautiful! And I did not understand what your look was saying, but I knew that I wanted so so much to be so close to you and never to have you let go of me and never let go of you. I wanted that moment to last forever.

And you said: "Thank you."

20

I love you. Please know that. Please always let today tell you if I love you. Don't ask yesterday. How can I speak to you out of yesterday? How can I love you but today? Please listen to my love today every day. I love you. And there is no other day but today. And today I love you always.

21

There is nothing partial about our loving. We find infinity in one another. That's what it is. In our love, I stare at the stars, and they are all a part of our love, and our love's world. And I walk across the fields our love has made, and the grass is tall, and the wild flowers are so beautiful and fragrant, and the sun shines brightly, and the birds dart to and fro, calling—and the dragonflies and the damselflies—and the butterflies—and the water tumbling over the rocks, making beautiful sounds. And all is music. And all is infinite. And all is you! And I love you!

I love you!

And you said I'm the only one who has ever made you feel like you are beautiful. But I have thought that for so long. That's the only impression I've ever had of you—that you are so beautiful.

When I lived next to you—I would hear you playing guitar and singing a Joan Baez song—"Diamonds and Rust"—and it was beautiful. I wanted to stop whatever I was doing and listen to you.

And at the picnic when you said "Children are like wild animals: you raise them and set them free"—it was so beautiful, and you seemed so wonderful to me. And I wanted to talk with you. And I saw you holding the baby, so lovingly.

I love being close to you, and looking at you. I love those moments so much. It is so real, and so wonderful, and I am so amazed that you are here so beautifully at the center of my life.

22

This room is becoming sacred to me. My home. The table where our candle burns each time we say "I love you."

This room: let our love rule this small kingdom, here where we meet and touch, and live!

Here I will write and I will sing, and we will sing and we will love. And in this place we will make a perfect world, a perfect life, composed in perfect love. And in the strength of that love, I will be able to take this room, this life, with me each time I must travel into the empty world, and still I will live, in spite of the blankness. Because the words you have poured into me will sustain me there, as they already do. And here, I will do my best to compose words that will sustain you in the times when we cannot touch except in our hearts and memory. And this room will be my gift to you. Our shrine. And I will live here.

You said I didn't say a word last night. And, for most of it, I don't think the possibility of saying something with my voice was even there. My mind was totally oblivious to the idea of words that I would speak. I was so focused on touching you, and kissing you, and hearing you, and feeling every movement you made and every touch you gave to me. I was so totally engrossed in all of that that I wasn't thinking a single word that could be said with my voice. I was just loving you.

And you said someone as smart as me could fake it. And I said someone as smart as you would know if it was fake.

Our loving says so much, and is expressed with such beauty, and spontaneity. I don't think it's possible for it to be faked, calculated but unfelt. I mean—I don't know how anyone could do it—because it's so creative, and so full of love and life. And that's what moves in us each time: the love, and the life that wants the love to be expressed, and felt. We love, and the love is felt. It is received. It's such a miracle! Every bit of love we give to each other is received. Nothing is lost, nothing left given but unreceived. And so, all of our love is fruitful. And we create our lives, and live fully in one another, in our love. And our love is our world.

And the other day you thought the parting didn't bother me as much as it bothers—hurts—you. When you think that way, you start feeling that I don't really love you,

43

and that you've been fooling yourself, and that it would be best for you not to get too close to me from now on.

It's not that it doesn't bother me to see you go each time. But, I do think it's easier for me, since I come back here and get into the same bed where we loved moments before, still warm with your warmth and mine. And I think I do not lose you in the same way you lose me at the moment when we part. Because I return to the place where we've been all evening, and all the feelings stay with me. Whereas, you have to bundle up and go out into the cold and the wind and the snow. I mean, you really have to go away from every image of our love, whereas I can look at the candle and our glasses of amaretto. It's less of a shock for me than what you have to go through.

It's not that you leaving doesn't hurt me. I miss you immediately. But there's more of you still with me, in this room, than there is of me that you can take with you when you go. Because you go to a different bed, in a different house, far across the cold winter from our love's bed...

23

You are so wonderful to me. You give me everything so beautifully! And you told me "thank you," and that I had made your dream come true! And you are my dream coming true every moment and every day and with every word and every kiss and every emblem you give me of your life. I love you so, so deeply. The feeling you give to me is so beyond description—so beautiful, so rich, so alive, so wonderfully fulfilled, like all the dreams that have ever been dreamed coming true. I am in heaven. That is what it felt like last night. Paradise. That's what you give me. Images of Paradise.

And five years ago I had visions of the creation of the universe—but it was just a structure, and terribly austere. But now, you have remade all my visions, and filled them with life, that I feel with every part of me, not just my mind. You have given me the real world that those visions were mere images of—a world filled with light and life. Thank you!

You love me into life—and I love you! I don't know what else to say. Everything I have is yours! Every vision, every word, every music that God has given me—I want to give it all to you—and I'm going to try. That's all I'm going to do for the rest of my life: find every possible way of giving everything to you. Because you are already giving everything I have dreamed of—and so much more!—to me. You give me so much that my old dreams are inadequate. And you show me such beautiful worlds that my dreams now fly freely across the sky, knowing that every dream is possible, and every dream is real. I love you! Because you are the one who has set my dreams free! And that's what I want to do for you: let you dream limitless dreams, knowing they are all real. I love you!

24

We danced Saturday. I love dancing with you. So beautiful! And you sang to me. I feel so—I feel your love so, so beautifully when you sing to me...

You gave me so much. You give me so much. I slept so deeply. It amazes me. But still I'm not surprised—I'm not surprised that your love could do that to me—calm me so much that I would sleep so deeply, with you. You calm every restlessness in me. You make me placid, yet fruitful. There are no storms in me when you are near—just life creating each new day, each new life. I love you forever. And the forever in me loves you.

That is why nothing else matters to me but you—and what I can make for you—vessels which I may give to you, into which I have poured my life and my love. That's all I want to make for the rest of my life: vessels, from which you may sip my love. Eternal vessels. A cup. A chalice. All containing the words "I love you Dale"—my Dale, my All, my Life, my Everything. I love you—and I'm going to use every gift God has given me to express that love, and to give it to you—forever. Because you have given me everything. And everything can't help but create another everything. And that's what I want to give. That's what I try to give you. And if you feel my love, then I am at least being partially successful. But—one day, I dream that the everythings we give will never end.

You said, Thursday, that for the first time you really felt that you wanted to be married to me—that you wanted to wake up with me, make lunches for me when I go to work—I love you so! Yes, I want to be married to you, too! I want to be with you always, and to give to you always, and to make life with you always.

25

Then, somehow—we touched. And it must have been pure desire to touch that led us to one another—because surely I didn't know where to turn, except to try to find you. And you must have wanted me to find you, or else it never could have happened...

And we found each other. And that was one of the darknesses you felt would always keep you separate from me—a part of you I could never know—

I love you—not just what you give me, or your joy. It is you I love—just like when you say to me, simply, "you"—

And we talked about the creation of the universe.

And you told me, on Friday, that you had never felt closer to me than those moments, after I had found you—and still, it was you who had found me. Because you were in the dark, and I could never find you by myself. You had to come to me when I was close to you—or else I never could have found you—because in your darkness I could not see you—because I had never been to that place before.

But—if you call me, I will always come. No matter where you are, if somehow you can reach out to me enough for me to know that you are calling to me, and that you need me to come to you, I will always come. I will always try to find you.

Because you have found me, and given me everything. And you always come to me, and lift me out of my darkness when work, or whatever, shadows my soul—and hides me from the real me. You love me, and my love reaches out to you—and I am whole again.

And I will always reach out to you...

Bathe me in your love! You said that's what you want to do! I love you!

26

You said that I need you, and that's okay. And I do need you. I need you always to be who you are. Because the real you gives to me so much more than every life and every dream I've ever imagined. Please do not feel you have to sacrifice your life, to meet mere material needs. Because if you sacrifice your dream, you take mine too— because they are one—

I love you. Please do not be afraid to let me help preserve the everything life that you give to me. Please let me give to you everything that life has given me to give. I love you everywhere, and in every way.

27

I do not blossom except in our love. And my life is not fruitful except in our love—because our love is the deepest, fullest river inside me—it is the source of all the other rivers. And to choose not to live in that innermost water, which makes our lives in one another, is to choose not to love anyone as much as I could love them. Because it is in our deepest love that I am most real—and one can only give reality. That's all love is: real life given. And if you don't pursue the most real life inside you, then you don't have that most real life to give, and all your loving suffers.

What I gave to others before was only the faith and hope that was in my dreams. But now my dream is here, living in this world outside of me—my dream has come to me both inside me and outside of me. And I am bathed in my dream, in our dream, in your love—and my love for you flows into the world, and loves everyone I love. And every love I have is a branch of the love I have for you. And that love feeds all my loves...

My life, the life I want to live, the life I have to live to be fully me, fully alive, is with you. Your love, and my love— our love together—that's what makes the real me. And all I ever wanted was to be real. And you give me that both in your giving and in your beautiful receiving of everything I give to you. You are the only one who receives everything I give. And I think I receive everything you give, too. And in that perfect receiving, our coffers are filled to overflowing, and we are left able to give all to everyone we love.

28

We live in a song—and the song will grow deeper and richer and more beautiful and perfectly resonant as our lives merge more and more into perfect oneness—not oneness of selves, but oneness of love, oneness of the life we will feel bearing us ever upward. It is that one shared life that will create perfection in everything we do and see. And we will hear music in everything, because our love will give to us a perfect hearing, and with that perfect hearing we will live in harmony with the beating of the earth. And we will give that hearing and that beating heart to others, that they may live as we have lived. And our lives will be fulfilled.

What have I said to you? What have you said to me?

"I love you." Do we not always say that, in everything we do? You said to me last night: "I'm going to give you so much." And I thought: "How can you possibly give me more than you already do?"

But, today our giving is perfect in desire to give. And it is perfect desire that leads to perfect life. Nothing else can bring one to perfection—only perfect desire. And our desire to love one another perfectly is perfect. And so, one day our loving, our giving, our sharing will be perfect. And our giving will contain everything, and there will be no pauses, no separations.

We will sing, and love will be our song, wending its way among the trees, sun-dappled morning breeze: I love you, Dale!

29

Universe. That is what our lives express. One song. One poetry. For, our words so perfectly match each other's soul visions. That is why I so often write with your words—because, they are a window in which I see the soul world just as clearly as when I peer into my own window words. We share *that* deeply! So deeply! That is where our love is founded. In the bottomless, endless, timeless abyss that is the ground of the entire universe as well as the beginning of every human soul. That is where we meet, and hold hands. It is that universe, and that music, that we face, in oneness of intent, so deeply inside our lives. That abyss, that light—that is where our love lives.

30

If only you could know that I am always perfectly desiring to be with you. I know I am not perfect—I do not live perfectly. But my desire is perfect. And perfect life *really is* born out of perfect desire. I know my inward desire is perfect. That inner perfection just hasn't perfectly transcended my outward self—and there are gaps, where sometimes an unborn portion of my self meets up with the need to love you—and it simply can't do it yet, because it hasn't been born yet.

But—I learn. And when I find I did not love you—my only desire is to somehow claim back that part of me that didn't love you, that I didn't give to you—and find it, and find how it is that that part of me wasn't alive and loving when life called it to love—and I want to shake that part of me into awakeness and say: "Hey! Why are you sleeping? Is this not your time for living? Is this not the moment you were created for? To love at this very moment? To create this moment's life? Why do you sleep, and let emptiness and ghosts roam the world where you should be living?"

I will shake every part of me to awakeness—and every part of me will be singing "I love you" to you—just please don't listen to ghosts. Don't ever believe that love is impossible. Don't ever believe there are limits. Please know always that all emptinesses are reclaimable, and that all the love and life that was ever created will be lived. No—the universe is not a seamless light and life. People look away from the light, and emptinesses travel across the universe, colliding with every lover, and sometimes momentarily blowing away the world their love has engendered. But, the fountain does not cease— life is infused forever—and none of it is lost—all can be lived, every apparent loss regained.

And the love I did not give you last night can be given to you today, along with the love that was made for today too. Because the love that I would have given you yesterday isn't lost—it just slept in a part of me that should have, but didn't, waken when life called it to give

51

its love, its reality, to the universe—to you, my true universe.

And now the dumb beast is awake, and ready to give. Please scatter the ghosts and come to the fountain. Life is waiting for us.

I love you!

31

You saw a galaxy—stars shining in the sky inside you, in our world. And I see what you describe in listening to you describe it—but it is not the same seeing. Still, I think I feel the same feeling that you feel in those moments.

I see other things, along the way, when we love. I always see a river, and a sparkling waterfall. And we walk up the shore toward the waterfall. And the waterfall is all light, all life, pouring into our world—all love. And we step into the waterfall and are made shimmering like the water itself, like this life.

And after, you look up and see light. And I must be looking at you as we lie upon the shores, and you stare up into the skies and see another reflection of the love we have been blessed with—

And every "I love you" has become a star.

32

Together our lives are a garden, out of which bloom the most beautiful flowers and fruits—and our loving is like water that makes the clay of which we were molded into the bearer of all living and all light. And without that water we were merely all potential—but in loving each other, all those possible lives become actual—we live everything—and the world lives everything in us—

I need you—just as life needs itself. And that is the way you need me too. That's why any clinging isn't bad for us—we reach out for each other when we feel ourselves falling away from life.

And life will always enable us to catch and hold each other when one of us is falling—so long as we always seek that holding and being near one another. Because the only thing that could keep us apart would be giving in to something untrue which told us not to desire to be together. And all untrue things will tell us that—they'll say "It can't work out—the world's just not that way."

But—no matter what way the world is, Life *is* that way—our truest feeling is desire to be with each other in every way. And that desire can overcome everything untrue.

I will come to you always, Dale. Forever I will be coming to you, loving you always, forever. I love you—my love. My life. My heaven. Stay with me forever!

33

My Dale—it truly is the mystical center of all life that we reach when we take our loving, which is our living, to its very center. I see that so clearly in what you wrote—and I had felt it so clearly in my own perceptions of where we are, where we travel together—but now I see in your words that same experience that I first tasted in a limited way over five years ago—I saw it then, just a glimpse, just enough to make me know it had to be real, just enough for me never to be willing to stop looking for that life— the life which now I not only see, but live. We live it!

And what is it? That gently breathing Time inside us that you so perfectly describe—that one inflowing, which unites all our life, then spills into the universe, lighting it with the same eternal light that our days and moments breathe into us.

Then, five years ago—I *saw* so much, conceptualized— and I was captivated by it all, but a few days later I had the words that had named what I had seen, but the feeling was gone. It was something that I knew existed, from first-hand experience—but I didn't have and couldn't get a hold of it again.

I tried so many things, looking for that world—wanting it to become my life, not just a vision. I tried reading the same books over—but they had become internalized, and did not produce a second awakening. It was like little Veronica—for three days I was privileged to walk through a magic kingdom—but to see it, not really to live it—because what I was seeing, this life that we share now, was so far over my head at that point, so far beyond who I was at that moment—for three days I walked through that kingdom, gazing, but not really touching— then the curtain fell, and for years I tried "to get it to happen again" (exactly how I described it)—I tried to study, I tried becoming a monk in worship of the Holy Spirit—but it didn't happen again. Because it wasn't something for me to hoard as my own possession—and that's exactly the way I treated it—I became a spiritual materialist—I was greedy for soul light—and thus, my life was filled with contradictions...

But you—it is here, in life—it is no longer something I see. It is a wide path I walk on with you, hand in hand. And with each step Life breathes into us. Yes, you are so right—it is Time itself that breathes inside us—our loving is one with the loving that created this entire universe. We become pure life in those moments—what I called the castle—I feel like I am walking into the very center of your life, of you, into a place beyond and within all faces, where you live in pure, naked love. And I feel you calling to me, calling me to come to the fountain, the river of life that bathes that world.

And I come to you.

You asked me once about Eden—what I thought about it—if it was a real place, where it is—

When that light pours in across our sky, creating the heavens before our eyes, with light that shines outward from within us—there we begin to live in Eden. Because that light, I believe, is the light that shines from Eden into this curtained world. And when we come to that place, and drop all complications of our earthly personality, and live in one loving essence—then, that light, that beautifully beating, breathing, ushing light raises us into Eden by wrapping us in the images, the world, the life that simply is, forever, Eden.

Eden Morning

Wedding

We are married! Forever! Because, we have wedded our lives. And today, that kind, old woman, who knows marriage in years of being married—today she helped us proclaim that inward wedding that we have felt so strongly for months and months—yet which we have wanted and needed for our entire lives—because: this wedding is who we are.

My home. Finally I am home—and my real life is beginning—I am living it now, everything that life has ever promised me in my dreams or visions or hope. My home. So deeply within you I desire to live, to stay, always. And I want you to come forever into me, into my soul, into my life, into the garden your love is making bloom.

Truth

What do I feel now that we are "married"—that a gap has been filled with the truth, with light. Before today, the world claimed that we were not wedded. Now it gives us a name that matches the life we are living: "married."

Ceremony

The ceremony was beautiful! So unexpected! Not at all just a simple legal proclamation. I felt myself being lifted and lightened and awed by the beauty of what we are living, this living wedding of our lives.

Every Day

That's why it still—the word "wedding" is what I feel when I think about our entire lives. My mind doesn't want that word to be confined to one day or one hour—I feel it flowing so naturally, so purely, so freely, every day, every time we touch, every moment when we are close. Our wedding! Blessed living weddedness in our lives! I love you, Dale!

Who I Am

You asked me not to do this—marry you—unless I was sure, unless I knew it was forever. I do know that. When I am with you, when I feel myself wrapped in your love, I am everything I always knew and dreamed myself to be. And, I used to tell people who I thought I was, who I thought I would one day be, when I was freed from my prisons—and some of them would call it "dreams," of the sort one wishes for. And I would say: "*No*—these are not dreams. These are who I am, and if I do not become this life, then I will have failed entirely"—

But I was imprisoned. And no one could know me, no one could understand.

But you—you reached into me, melted away every limit, touched me—kissed me, and I waked and became who I am, alive. And you came into my center—there is a home in me for you, too. My center, my soul, will forever rain my life across the skies, loving you, wanting only to find you, wanting only for you to know me everywhere, in everything.

Revelation

My one desire, my one need—has always been to reveal everything, every life in me—to give it all to one person, who could understand it, and *live* it with me. That's what I always wanted and needed—to be able to share and live together with my perfect complement every creation, every vision, every life—to perfectly communicate every life inside me. To perfectly share. To have someone here at the center of our one universe, watching the skies unfold their radiant imagery.

And yes, I have found that one love—the one who came to me, the one who needed everything I am to become herself. That's what I thought I'd never find—someone who needed *all* of me.

But you—you *do* need all of me—you need *me*, you want *me*, you love *me*! I'll never be alone—because when we touch, we touch everywhere, and there is no part of us that is not touching, no part of us that is not communicating its entire being and receiving in return a love that comes from the deepest river inside us.

The Shore

We live on that shore—"the ocean of marriage" she
said—yes, my beautiful ocean—that was in those visions
six years ago! I was going to leave the land and walk into
the ocean, into my new, radiant, true life! With the sun
shining above—that's what I was seeing! I never knew
what the ocean was before in that vision—the sun I
associated with life in my soul, but the ocean I didn't
understand—but, now I see! Yes, my love! I am holding
your hand—it is a beautiful, calm day, with the sun, that
river of light, flowing inside us, shining, lighting the
universe for us to see all, reveal all that love can see and
live!

My darling—sail with me forever! Yes, I am fulfilled!
Every promise is today fulfilled. I am wedded! Wedded
to life! My life I drink in the love you pour over me, into
me!

This Day

My dove! My angel! My light! Shine with me forever!
This day is the holiest of my life, the most cherished, the
most eternal, the most living. Because, it contains in one
day the word I will live forever, the word I want to see
with you forever, revealing forever every light. My love,
this day gives us this word forever, this sacred, radiant
word, this sacred, holy life, this one word: wedding.

I love you forever! My Dale!

I will!

Yes!!

Creativity and Love

I see both of our lives beginning to flow freely—creativity spinning out from the deep and fulfilled living we share and give to one another.

You saw it in my story—that everything is there in the story, all the feelings and ideas and imaginings that are closest to my center, my striving for life. But then, you said that there is one other place where all that I am comes to life and expression: in our loving.

Yes—that is my true center! Our loving. That is the star forever burning at the center of all my life, all my work, all my creation. It is our love that will live in every work I create. It is our love that carries me through each day when I must go away from you.

The Car

I was so afraid at first—I dreamed of being in a car with you, your car, with me driving—and the car went off the road into a forest, and I couldn't steer it or stop it—but somehow, the trees moved out of the way, and I wasn't hurt.

And when I felt myself moving so quickly—it was such a change to be moving in a single direction that it felt like I was moving so fast—

But the forest became this ocean where we now live—so expansive, sun laden.

I love you, Dale!

This Life

This life is such a beautiful ocean—so wide, so all encompassing. It's so unbelievable, so beautiful! That one symbol, today, at our wedding, brings together the dangling ends of every dream and longing vision I've ever had. In my simplistic novel, I wanted to "bathe in the sea"—but then I could not see that the ocean I wanted was your love. I only knew that, from where I stood then, seven years ago, what I wanted and needed and longed for looked like an ocean.

And now, today—I am given that ocean, that sea, that seeing, that life!

Birth

And we move so quickly into life—quickly, just as life itself is a river flowing, ever changing, yet always centered in light. So, we now ray our light, the light that flows into us at our center, which together we bear into the world, watching it be born into us when we love, in our love.

I Will Come to You

My love, I am home. I am here, with you, forever. I am yours forever, and I will come to you always, always loving, with all my life.

Everything that you know in me, you know—because I have always given you everything, my entire self. And in our loving—that is where I live the highest life I can live. And you should never doubt me—please never doubt my love. Because there is nothing left behind when I love you.

You always want me to come to you—and I always want to come to you. I always need you. And you need me.

Your Love

And—I know that you give to me your entire heart and soul, all your love. You take me there. I feel myself being drawn in, I feel my ice, all my crusty thoughts, melting into pure awareness and sensation of your presence, your love, your wanting me to be with you, your needing me, asking me to come closer to you, to share everything, to see the same galaxies, the same light, to ride the same beams of light across the universe...

You ask me to come to you, to come with you.

Kiss

And you came to get me, you came and found me when I didn't think it was possible—because of conventions, more ideas, more thoughts. You came to me, and kissed me—and your kiss, that first kiss, in the car—began to melt away all the walls, the clashing emptinesses that years of confused loneliness and suffering had built around me, which even my visions could not break through. Your kiss—you kissed me, and your love is the key to my entire life.

Promises

For years I drove around lonely roads high on rocky, barren terrain—my scattered visions which I tried to understand and tie together with intellectual musings—but none of it could work, because I was alone, far from my home.

They promised you to me—my highest imaginings, all those years—pointed to a life I could not understand then, but which I knew was my real life.

Beginning

This ocean world, this flowing love, this rivering light—my Dale, we live it at its beginning today. But, amazingly, as we grow, the fountain moves further inward, becomes yet more radiant, showers the universe with an ever increasing sparkled aura, ever brighter!

Your galaxies will bloom. We are at the beginning of our life, this path. Though we already see so far, across such beautiful fields—we will naturally fly higher—the waters welling in our hearts and souls will transform the world around us, and that world, responding to our life, will buoy us higher and higher, until the world and our dreams become one.

The World

I told you long ago that the world accommodates every life, that it necessarily adjusts. And perhaps we had too little faith then, and neither of us realized how true that is. But there will come a day when we will smile at those words as such a naive statement of the awesome power of life and love, the awesome living that centered, devoted love gives birth to.

We will live that loving forever, my Dale, my darling love, my opener of every door, my treasure, my wife!

I Love You, Dale

I dreamed of you so long ago:

Love ushing in the Eden morning,
Oceans welling, eternally born,
Voices singing all creatures to life.
Eden, indeed—but for me, a dream.

You lighted within me, butterfly!
Out of heart's deep night you have come,
Uttering life with your every word.

Dale! You are my soul afire!
All creation shines in you—
Lighting the way to all my dreams,
Eden welling: my love in you.

The Gateway

Toward a gateway framed in petals
you draw me—
I, who have walked a dust-ridden path,
and spent many nights lying on stones—
your sacred emblem beckons me.

I enter the castle:
warmth and life and song.
Your voice soothes me, caresses,
entices me to life.

You touch me deeply, and I am home.
I begin to see you where you live:
in perfect loving giving.
Softly you call me still.
I begin to see...

Song sparrows stir,
then dash across the sky.
The galaxies awakened sing.
Borne in a rushing ribbon of light
we melt in sparkles across the night,
and silent dew drops radiant on our life.

Love

Love is a river of light,
born within us,
from beyond the center of our being.

It flows through us,
asking us to live its life,
to make this earth in its image.

Before

Before I knew my love,
I knew a world that was dying, and
a heaven that was striving to be
but somehow couldn't find
its way into existence.

I knew what had to be, because
life has granted me vision.
But instead of making the world
become what I knew it was in truth,
my actions parted with
the light of my visions,
and I created for my home an
expansive universe pocked with
deathly emptiness.

I saw light coming in at the center, but
instead of living this truth into the world,
I often created Hell.
My mind was betraying my soul, and
the life I knew should have been
was becoming an aching death.

The Monks

Those who live alone do not know
the meaning of love on this earth.

The monks know God.
They find love
in the center of their souls,
shining out over them,
across the universe,
like an inward sun.
They feel the warmth of this sun.
Its love beckons them.
The monk who follows his light
finds truth, finds life.

But the life he finds is not that
of this earth, but of eternity in itself,
the paradise that has never fallen.
That is where he seeks to live.
That world is his goal.

But God did not create
this earth and humankind
solely that they would learn
to reject a corrupt world and
turn within to find Him.
He created this earth
to be paradise.

That same paradise
which the monks find within
is meant to live on earth as well.
The monks are not wrong to turn
to God within themselves:
for it is solely from within
that they are called.

Fear 1

There are those who have not found
the one they need,
but fear to leave the one they are with
out of fear of loneliness.

This is a trap that can only lead to greater
unhappiness than the loneliness itself.
One who fears loneliness
lacks the courage to be all that his soul
asks him to be.

One does not live in this world
without courage.
Truth cannot be lived
if one shuns difficulties.

Fear 2

Fear has no place in this world.
Life cannot be guided by fear.
Only death is guided by fear.

To live, to love, we must live
by our best, most faithful estimate
of where the path to truth lies.

Admittedly, it is our imperfect
judgment that we must live by.
Yet, living by judgment leads to
perfection.

Those who are ruled by fear always find
a world far worse than their worst fears.

Those who seek to avoid a suffering
that lies along the path of truth,
the path to life,
inevitably end up creating
for themselves and those who love them
a worse suffering
than that which they feared
and away from which they turned.

Deception

To accept an imperfect life
is to turn away from the path
leading to perfection and fulfillment.

To turn away from the path
that leads to true life
is to turn onto a road that
leads to darkness and sorrow and despair.

How can you give to someone
you know is not the one you need?
If you pretend to her that she is that one,
you have lied to her and not given
your entire self.

Thus, you cheat her of your true love,
and give her something that cannot possibly
help her to find the life her soul
has promised her.

If the deception is sufficiently flawless,
you guide her into a hell you create
for both her and yourself.

You have betrayed her too,
not just yourself.
You have made her also the victim of your
inadequacy.

And in the end, you realize that
it would have been far better
to have been honest from the start,
both with her and with yourself.

We lie to each other.
We lie to ourselves.

Suffering

A suffering which lies in
the path leading to life
is lit by the love that
draws the traveller
toward his end.

And though he may not see this light
at the time, in being the light of truth,
it is sufficient to sustain him in his trial.

But a suffering created by fear of life
contains no sustaining light,
because the suffering is shrouded
in its victim's fear and cowardice,
which created it.

It is not part of the path to life,
and so contains no sustenance,
unless through it the sufferer discovers
the error of his bowing to fear,
and so turns away from fear.

The Grandest Illusion

I wrote these words:

> *I burst upon the night-deep sky,*
> *Streaming star where there was none;*
> *Now my life is swallowed by*
> *The dark and scatter of my blood.*

A nova is born in a
spectacular blaze of light.
But it quickly collapses,
fades into a dim
white dwarf star,
engulfed by an ever-expanding shell
of dark star matter
that gives off
no light
of its own.

This was my blood:
the light that should have been,
but somehow had failed to come to be.

All those who give up
the search for the beloved end
in this condition.
They are meant to love on this earth,
but have given in to despair
and now lack faith,
doubting even that their beloved exists.
They cannot find anything in themselves,
even if they have been granted
a clear vision of what is meant to be,
because they have given up hope.
They have decided the universe is not perfect,
after all,
that all their visions
of love and joy were illusions.

Yet this belief itself
is the grandest illusion
of all. It is the one lie
that makes all lies believable.

Shadowland

We cannot be what we are
unless we have our center.
Lovers cannot be who they are meant to be
unless they first find their beloved.

She is the key.
He is the key.

Either all doors will be unlocked,
or all will remain closed.

Either a lover will faithfully persevere,
searching every last corner of the universe
until he finds the one he needs,
or despair will defeat love's purpose,
and an entire life will be spent
in a shadowland.

Indeed, many in the shadowland are deemed
wonderful successes by the world.
They put what energy they have into
worldly labors,
because they have given up all of their
heart's and soul's desires.

But these people are not
what they could have been.
They do not change the world for the better.
They live on the talents of their
minds and bodies.

But these are nothing
compared to the genius
that would have been
had mind and body been united
with heart and soul,
all inspired by the light of
eternal fulfillment.

Earthly Love

Earthly love is a circle of light.
The light travels both ways
around the circle,
so that every creation is lighted
both from within and from without.

The sun shines within me,
just as it does for the monks.
But, for me, another sun shines,
lighting me from the outside too.
The sun within my love shines through her life
and into me.
And the light from her touches me
and warms me,
and I become everything the light within me
has always told me I must be.

The Path

My love and I walk
along a path by the river.
The shore is lit by the light of the waters,
but still we sometimes stumble and fall.
We are not perfect.

This is a path leading to paradise.
But only the perfect feel paradise
in every moment.
We know it is there in every moment, and
we know we are getting nearer to the peak
of this mountain,
nearer to the river's source.
But some moments we are lost,
and we rely on love and faith until
we find the path again.

Loving

I search for my love's center,
to love her there,
with the deepest love in me,
with the peak of my being,
so that she will know everywhere who I am
and what my love is.

I search
for the place in her where
all life flows into her, where
she ceases to recognize even her own being
because everything she sees is
love and light.

And that love flows into her
of its own accord.
And her first recognition is that
it is love for me,
born from a place beyond her, yet
flowing into her deeply, boundlessly,
and becoming her own.

It is me
loving her from beyond herself
that she feels—
me loving her from paradise,
where we were born,
where our souls shall always live,
with the love life has given us
to give to one another,
forever.

I Face My Love

I face my love,
and she is my light, my world.
In her is the fulfillment of my every need
and desire.

In giving her all, I have all.
In finding all for her, I gain all
that my heart and soul and mind and body
have ever needed to find.

I face my love,
and I am face to face with my life.

Epilogue

Tomorrow, when you wake, I will give this book to you—
twenty five years after that beautiful day on which we
became wedded in the eyes of the world—though we had
wedded within our love long before then. I do believe we
were intended to marry from the beginning of time, and
the events that guided our direction in life were intended
to help us find each other.

Our children are grown now, and have left the home we
made for them. You were the creator of the home, while I
labored endless hours to try to enable it, financially.

I asked you to be a certain kind of mother, and you
agreed—really, that is the only kind of mother you know
how to be—one more sign that our love was meant to be.
I thank you so so much for raising our children the way
you did. I am so blessed in having been able to share
parenting with you.

You devoted every energy and creativity within you
toward being the best, most completely loving mother
you could be—staying home to give them everything that
can possibly be given—including their education—such
that, being their mother became your identity.

Ah! You have struggled so to find a purpose, a meaning
for life, since their departure. And worse, suffered, since
the apparent reward for your sacrifice has at times been
disdain, dismissal, and even resentment. But that is
ending now, as they grow into their own lives, establish
their own relationship with the world, endeavor to move
it to suit their needs. In retrospect, the life we gave them
begins to seem less worthy of their criticism...

At the lake, you turned to watch him swimming, and
then you turned back. And she was nowhere! And you

looked, and you looked, and you called to me—but I was far away, tending the grill. And, desperate, you turned, and turned, you looked, you searched, frantically. Where was she? Then, your eyes were pulled down. And there she was, face up beneath you, beneath the water, unmoving, eyes open, still, calmly looking up at you. And you lurched downward, pulled her up, gathered her into your arms, and she did not immediately respond. And you shook her, patted her back rapidly—and she coughed and began to breathe. And later she told you she had slipped and fallen under the water, and she didn't know what to do, so she waited.

She waited for you, trusting. And you were there. I love you for that moment, for being who you are. That one moment would have ended all, fractured Life irrevocably. But you reacted, found her, revived her, and life as it was meant to be proceeded. It is impossible to imagine what life would have been had you not been *you* at that specific moment.

And him, too. Didn't your actions that night prevent a catastrophe that would have denied him the possibility of living a life that includes happiness? Fighting the fever's advance, cradling him in your arms, wiping him down as he screamed, wanting only to calm him, make him inwardly feel your presence, your love, praying that your love could somehow be a barrier against whatever was happening, a shield.

You were alone that long night, as I drove your older son through a snow storm. You faced that night alone, just you and your trembling, screeching babe.

My love, your love *was* a barrier that night, and a healing force. You reached into him and blocked the advance of an insidious unknown. Your presence insulated his core from the ravaging attack, and he recovered.

We learned later what those sharp, high-pitched screams meant, how close he actually came to being among those who did not survive. And Dr. Joe wanted him never to have the pertussis again; nor her.

My love, it is because of you that the world has both of them today, because of you that they have themselves. Your love changed those horrorful moments into the possibility of life. You saved them, I know that's true.

As for me: we know now how many promises I did not keep. I was weaker than I thought. I am strong when I am able to come to you always, be with you always. But the stress of separation—I never became fully able to cope with that. And over the years, as the necessity grew for me to be increasingly apart from you, as I tried to provide the material aspects of what we both wanted for the children, I *did* fall in ways you are aware of only too well.

It's true, what Britomart says:

> *For knight to leave his Ladie were great shame,*
> *That faithfull is, and better were to die.*

Because if he dies before the unfaithful moment occurs, then at least all the life he gave to her was true. And that truth can continue to live inside her, and, to a degree, sustain her.

It's better that I didn't die. But, I wish...

I thought I would learn to carry your love with me into every darkness, and maintain my bearings, keep hold of the beauty of your love, let it sustain me no matter what I was facing. But, as the work piled up, forcing us to separate tasks, and opportunities to let the interior river flow into me dwindled, I *did* lose touch.

Oh, those dreams I would have! The bee nests filling our yard, tall mounds with hornets madly swirling round— and I had no way to eliminate the danger. Then, running as fast as I could down the road, out of breath, heart pounding, from the wolves that would kill me—taking your and the kids' financial livelihood away—only to see suddenly ahead of me an enormous wolf appear out of nowhere, rushing, leaping directly at my neck, head tilted sideways, jaws wide open—and the dream ends.

That's how my unconscious viewed my life.

When the crisis came where I realized it was possible that we could be homeless, living in a car, I rejected every desire in myself to maintain inner light, and life became a war I needed to survive just to provide you and the children with a place to live—more if possible—but I was not to care about having anything for myself. All was to be sacrifice.

But, for some reason, I'm not good at living an outward facing life of sacrifice. I bleed internally, I hemorrhage. I don't know why. It seems like I should be stronger, but...

I need a celebratory, sacramental life, centered in our wedding, in order to be whole. I need contact with you. Without you, I go crazy, I just don't know how to live.

Working an endless succession of seventy-five hour weeks to sometimes not even be able to pay all of our bills—and trying to give what little waking time was left to the kids—obstructed that possibility. And, through my own fault, my own weakness, I became isolated terribly, admitting into our life a different, excessive world, where I numbed myself with booze, to mute the spiritual pain, kept myself mechanically working into the deep night, then woke early the next day, asking coffee to prevent my eyes from closing as the bleak highways took me hours away from you.

Though the constancy of your love clothed me, both from within and without, I was withering, through my own fault—because I had intentionally turned from the living river, deeming that joy could not be afforded, given the dangerous possibilities economics had revealed. I became grimfaced; and that hurt you.

You were the bearer of my dying wounds. You suffered them. Yet your love remained strong and true throughout those times—while I flailed away, Cuchulainn-like, warring the raging waves.

Your love alone was my solace—though I did not deserve to receive it.

Your asthma—it would suffocate you at times. Did I do that to you? Because it was at the moments of my worst failings that the instances first came to you. Like you were suffocating within, gasping for breath interiorly— and your bodily nature was enacting that suffering in sympathy.

I am allergic to the world. But you bear my sins in your own suffering. It is a terrible thing. No one who was loved the way you have loved me should ever have had any falling whatsoever.

You rescued me again and again, throughout those long years. So, like Timias, I am compelled to ask:

> *What service may I do vnto thee meet,*
> *That hast from darkenesse me returnd to light,*
> *And with thy heauenly salues and med'cines*
> *sweete,*
> *Hast drest my sinfull wounds?*

Because it never was your fault, none of it should ever have happened.

Would that I could live today with sufficient honor to merit the title even of Arthur's squire! After I promised you so much more.

I am so blessed that you wanted me—and still do—you who can stand in the face of anything, everything, and still love permanently. I do love you. I have always loved you.

My love, I believe what I wrote to you more than twenty five years ago, on February 19:

> *And the love I did not give you last night can be given to you today, along with the love that was made for today too. Because the love that I would have given you yesterday isn't lost—it just slept in a part of me that should have, but didn't, waken when life called it to give its love, its reality, to the universe—to you, my true universe.*

Yes.

Writing this book has revealed to me the man I was when you first found me, and the man I became because of you. And it has resurrected a strength in me. I know that I am ready now to live with you better than I have ever since those early days. Every day, every moment.

In sane life, nature is tethered to the interior reality that is our beginning. It changes with time, and can be moved by love. The key to living, I think, is to close the distance between nature and its within—eliminate the spaces where shadows may creep in, distort, obscure, steal.

And no one changes in their core being. Our interior substance simply *is*. All that can change is the degree to which that inward silence is expressed into the world, through the accidental clothing we call our self.

82

Your love saturates my being when I am whole, makes all that is inside me brilliant! You deserve everything I ever promised. And I would justify your love today—live now and forevermore what was always meant to be.

I love being with you, in this world. I love these days we have been given. For so long, I hoped just to stay alive until the children were grown, I hoped I could be there for you for that long, to pay the bills at least. But we've been given more.

And part of our work now is creating on this land—our kingdom, you call it—a sustenance that will free us even more over time: our vegetable gardens, our berries, the mini orchard we've started. And your beautiful rock gardens! We are transforming this little world, creating a home for ourselves, a nest—an island of beauty and fulfillment for us, and a comforting place of peace and support that the children can visit and enjoy.

We are beginning to live the Earth-centered life that I've intended to describe in the third book. I hope we are given that entire life—and more! Yes, I want provision made by Life such that *all* the books can be written! For that to happen, we'll both have to live into very old age indeed. Healthy old age...

Whatever happens, I'm glad that Life allowed me to give you at least this one simple book. I am so privileged to have been able to share this much life with you. It is such a gift.

This book... oh, I hope you like it! I hope it reveals to you our love—its foundation, and also what we live today!

Remember the Arlo concert at Mohawk Mountain, when we were first together? I remember sitting on the quilt with you, close to the stage—so happy to be sharing that day with you! And during the first intermission, we walked around the stage, and saw Arlo wandering in a fenced area behind it. We called to him, and he approached. And we requested "Ocean Crossing." And at the very start of the next set, he turned to the band and said "Ocean Crossing"—which seemed to surprise them. And that moment, sitting close to you on the quilt, gazing at your beautiful face as you watched and listened, cradling your hand in mine, touching through the music, that song, the sunshine, the breeze, that day, was for me one of the truly beautiful moments in our beginning.

We have crossed a vast ocean together, indeed, hand in hand, in these twenty-five years...

I think often about how I will describe that ocean, in the book I have always promised, the book you asked me to write into that beautiful velvet diary, "the color of passion's blood," that you gave to me five years ago "in remembrance of true love." You gave it to me "for the golden glow of becoming one in Wedding." It waits in the drawer beside me where I write these words today. It waits for the day of its becoming.

I have tried to begin that becoming—the preparation for it—with this book. I promise you: I will pour every energy and imagination I am granted for the rest of my life into truly living the wedding that is the foundation of both our lives; and beyond that, into transcribing its being into an image that can be a sacred room within our life. And also, we hope, a lens through which others— those few who can still hear and see—may intuit the truth that wedding, as we have lived it, is. That objective, clearly stated in the early words, has not changed and never will. It's who I am. It's who you married. That me is still the same Kevin you loved from the start.

We'll have to go to the British Isles, you know—
Stonehenge, the Midlands, the unconquered western
shores, visit the Tor, the Isle of Avalon, Glendalough—
before *Wedding* can be written. What? They say Avalon
isn't a real place? Oh, we'll find it!

Ah! My mind keeps going back to that lovely morning in
Victoria, when I suddenly woke after an hour or two of
sleep, after we had loved so beautifully. The imprint of
your love was fresh on my soul and body and mind, and
in my spirit. And those words came to me, which I
scribbled onto that tiny piece of paper I have held closely
ever since:

> *I conceived this telling of these events...*

Conception: the beginning of my own rebirth into the
truth of our love.

And a few months later, on your birthday, I indeed took
up my spectacles and quill, gathered all the old pages,
and began the study and retelling of our beginning that
is this book.

And tomorrow, the twenty-fifth anniversary of the day
we became wedded in the eyes of the world, I will give
these words to you. I give them to you forever, my love. I
love you forever. I love you!

Oh, that Victoria night! It shimmers inside me, sweet,
luminous! You wakened me so powerfully! My beautiful
Dale! My sweet valley. Thank you so much for loving me!

Long ago, when I was still in the hospital, on July 19, at
10:30 in the evening, you wrote these words:

> *Kevin darling—I am listening to our tape—*
> *October 31st—nine whole months ago—we have*
> *come so far—and yet, the beauty, the simplicity*

*of our sweet harmony, the natural joy and
vitality was always there. I just said on the tape:
"it's neat when you can do something and it just
happens because it's part of you." Yes! Oh yes—it
is hard for me to believe that as we were singing
these songs and laughing and sharing soft,
loving words, we had not yet loved one another
totally—did we know as we were singing those
tender songs that night that it would indeed be
that very night that we would give ourselves to
one another completely? Did we feel it as we
were singing "I want you, I need you, I love
you"? I can't remember—but I know that I must
have wanted that to be the night—I know I must
have wanted to give myself to you forever.*

*You just called—and we are just so funny—
neither of us could say goodbye—we just kept
throwing our words back and forth to one
another—like kisses that feel so wonderful that
you just don't want them to end—*

*Today in your writing you said you have never
felt so whole—so strong—so powerful... and you
said that I have given this to you—that my love
has gathered up all the pieces of you that lay
scattered and torn across the universe—but
really, we have given that to each other—it is a
divine and purposeful union...*

*I don't know why, but tonight I have been
thinking about the legend of 'the Sword in the
Stone.' Remember how strong and mighty men—
warriors really—came from near and far to try
and pull the Sword from that Stone (and thereby
become King of England)? They clenched their
mighty fists about it, and with all the force they
could find within every muscle they pulled and
tugged and wrenched and screamed—and went*

86

away in despair, for the sword still stood within its stony encasement. And then came Arthur, a young man, not much more than a boy, small of frame and shy of manner. Gently, he wrapped his fingers around the hilt of that beautiful sword—almost timidly, it is said, for he knew not why he did it and had no expectations or design—he touched that sword and held it—and something wondrous occurred! That Sword was lifted up by him as easily as if the stone had melted—and they stood there, King and Sword— shining. And all were amazed.

And that's how I feel... that in a world of pullers and tuggers and wrenchers and screamers, something held me fast within my fortress— something kept me strong and still, awaiting the one, the only one, who would touch me, really <u>touch</u> me, with the light of his eyes, the words of his mind, the love of his heart, the beauty of his soul, with all this and more—who would touch me gently and carefully—bringing me to life... bringing us to life—to this, our life.

It is exactly midnight. Exactly! And I said I would sleep at midnight—and I will.

With you... my love.

Let me be that man for you again, my love! I am ready.

The first book, so long promised, is now accomplished. And I know you know it is true. Now I will put down my quill, and come to you, rejoin you in real life. Forever.

13 August 2009

87

Prayer

I am here, Love!
And shall ever be:
Your creation.

See our love, Dale:
Embrillianced lake,
Silent, still.

And hear:
Ever these words
Are *thine* art.

www.ingramcontent.com/pod-product-compliance
Lightning Source LLC
Chambersburg PA
CBHW031856170626
46807CB00004B/1762